This Little Tiger book belongs to:

_____

_____

_____

_____

KT-154-864

For Sarah and Benjamin
J.W.

For George
T.W.

LITTLE TIGER PRESS
An imprint of Magi Publications
1 The Coda Centre, 189 Munster Road, London SW6 6AW
www.littletigerpress.com
First published in Great Britain 1999
This edition published 1999
Text copyright © Judy West 1999
Illustrations copyright © Tim Warnes 1999
Judy West and Tim Warnes have asserted their rights to be
identified as the author and illustrator of this work under
the Copyright, Designs and Patents Act, 1988
A CIP catalogue record for this book is available from
the British Library
All rights reserved · ISBN 1 85430 624 3 · Printed in China
5 7 9 10 8 6

Have you got my Purr?

by
Judy West and Tim Warnes

LITTLE TIGER PRESS
London

"Oh Mummy, Mummy!"
"What's the matter, little Kitten?
Why are you crying?"
"Oh Mummy, Mummy, I've lost my purr."
"You'll find your purr, little Kitten.
Just wait and see."

"Oh Dog, Dog, have you got my purr?"
"Woof, woof," said Dog, licking his bone.
"I haven't got your purr, little Kitten.
This is my *woof*. Why don't you ask Cow?"

"Oh Cow, Cow, have you got my purr?"
"Moo, moo," said Cow, flicking flies with her ears.

"I haven't got your purr, little Kitten. This is my *moo*. Why don't you ask Pig?"

"Oh Pig, Pig, have you got my purr?"
"Oink, oink," said Pig, snuffling
in the straw.

"Oh Duck, Duck, have you got my purr?"
"Quack, quack," said Duck, splashing in the water.

"I haven't got your purr, little Kitten. This is my *quack*. Why don't you ask Mouse?"

"Oh Mouse, Mouse, have you got my purr?"
"Squeak, squeak," said Mouse, nibbling cheese
in the barn. "I haven't got your purr, little Kitten.
This is my *squeak*. Why don't you ask Sheep?"

SQUEAK SQUEAK

"Oh Sheep, Sheep, have you got my purr?"
"Baa, baa," said Sheep, munching grass in
the field. "I haven't got your purr, little Kitten.
This is my *baa*. Why don't you ask wise old Owl?"

"Wise old Owl, have you got my purr?"
"Hoot, hoot," said the wise old Owl, blinking his big round eyes.

"I haven't got your purr, little Kitten.
This is my *hoot*. Why don't you go
back and ask your mother?"

"Oh, Mummy, Mummy," wailed little Kitten. "*Nobody's* got my purr. Dog hasn't got it. He's got a woof. Cow hasn't got it. She's got a moo. Pig hasn't got it. She's got an oink. Duck hasn't got it. She's got a quack. Mouse hasn't got it. He's got a squeak. Sheep hasn't got it. She's got a baa. Wise old Owl hasn't got it. He's got a hoot. Oh, Mummy, Mummy, I've lost my purr!"

"You haven't lost your purr, little Kitten. Come here and I'll explain.

"Nobody's got your purr.
Your purr is inside you
when you're happy!
Listen, little Kitten,
listen . . ."

"My *purr!*
Oh, Mummy.
I've found my purr!
It was here
all the time."
So little Kitten
curled up . . .

and purred and purred
and purred.

PURR PURR

Curl up with a book from Little Tiger Press

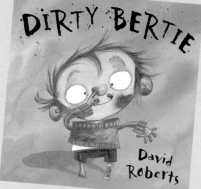

DIRTY BERTIE

David Roberts

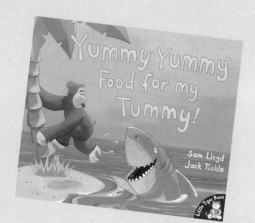

Yummy Yummy Food for my Tummy!

Sam Lloyd
Jack Tickle

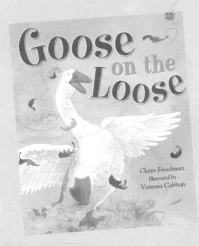

Goose on the Loose

Claire Freedman
Illustrated by
Vanessa Cabban

Careful, Santa!

Julie Sykes
Tim Warnes

The Very Ugly Bug

Liz Pichon

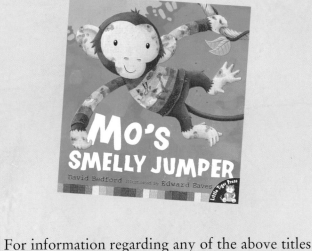

MO'S SMELLY JUMPER

David Bedford illustrated by Edward Eaves

For information regarding any of the above titles or for our catalogue, please contact us:
Little Tiger Press, 1 The Coda Centre,
189 Munster Road, London SW6 6AW
Tel: 020 7385 6333 Fax: 020 7385 7333
Email: info@littletiger.co.uk
www.littletigerpress.com